Samuel French Acting Edition

I0591770

A Little Something for the Ducks

and

Scent of Honeysuckle

by Jean Lenox Toddie

SAMUELFRENCH.COM   SAMUELFRENCH.CO.UK

Please refer to page 46 for further copyright information.

A Little Something for the Ducks

CAST

Irma

Samuel

A LITTLE SOMETHING
FOR THE DUCKS

SCENE: The grounds of a senior citizens' housing complex.

TIME: Today.

> *The stage is empty except for a bright yellow bench left of center and facing the audience and a yellow trash can down left. A yellow sign is suspended from a wire, its black letters admonishing, "Don't Feed The Ducks."*
>
> *As the lights rise IRMA is sitting on the bench.*
>
> *Elderly and energetic, she is wearing a soft gray suit and black shoes. A yellow scarf is tied around her neck and a yellow hat perched on her head. She removes spotless white gloves and lays them on the black purse she holds in her lap. Hands folded, she is looking straight ahead as Samuel enters.*
>
> *SAMUEL, also elderly, is dressed in a gray suit. He is wearing black shoes and a yellow tie. He carries a paper bag.*

Both SAMUEL and IRMA have the ageless quality of the very old, so the age of the actors is unimportant. If younger performers play the parts, it is suggested they avoid obvious makeup and suggest age by subtle whitening of eyebrows and hair and by moving with the cautiousness of the elderly. The performers, whether youthful or mature, should avoid caricature, juxtaposing the characters' somewhat comic aspects with gentle inner dignity.

.As SAMUEL enters, he walks center stage, whistling thinly the old tune, "Wait Till The Sun Shines, Nellie." He stops, contemplates the audience with affection, opens his bag and begins to scatter imaginary bread on the ground in front of him. It becomes obvious that the area where the audience is sitting is a pond and SAMUEL is feeding the ducks.

IRMA. (*without so much as a glance at SAMUEL*) Don't feed the ducks!

SAMUEL. (*stops, stands motionless for a moment, turns*) Eh?

IRMA. (*looking straight ahead*) Don't feed the ducks. The sign says don't feed the ducks.

SAMUEL. It's alright. I've been feeding the ducks for years and no one ever objected. (*He begins to scatter the bread again, hesitates, turns and tips his hat. He then moves down stage right, scattering the bread.*) Eh, Nellie, you pig! Always pushing everyone else out of the way. No manners, no manners! (*He stamps a stiff old leg to send the unseen Nellie running.*)

IRMA. (*shifting slightly on the bench but still not glancing at SAMUEL*) You'll be arrested.

SAMUEL. Seven years I've been feeding the ducks and I've never been arrested.

IRMA. Just because you've been lucky, you should act like a criminal? (*points to the sign*) Don't feed the ducks!

SAMUEL. (*contemplates the sign*) That means you shouldn't throw the bread in the water. You throw the bread in the water you got pollution. I don't throw the bread in the water, I throw it on the grass. (*He tips his hat and turns back to the ducks.*) Here you are. You, you there, come on . . . Not you, Nellie. Get away!

IRMA. So why shouldn't she have some bread?

SAMUEL. She's had enough already.

IRMA. She wants more. She's hungry.

SAMUEL. She doesn't need anymore.

IRMA. (*imitating SAMUEL, without yet having glanced at him*) "She doesn't need any more." She's bigger than the rest. She needs more.

SAMUEL. She's bigger than the rest because she's a pig. (*to Nellie*) Shoo!

IRMA. (*to Nellie*) The criminal knows everything. He says you've had enough.

SAMUEL. (*irritated, he approaches IRMA*) She's hungry? You think she's hungry? Here, you feed her! (*He thrusts the bag into IRMA's hand.*)

IRMA. (*Equally irritated, she contemplates the bag, then impulsively reaches into it and throws a piece of bread to Nellie.*) Here!

SAMUEL. Eh! Don't feed the ducks!

IRMA. (*startled*) What?

SAMUEL. (*with satisfaction*) The sign says don't feed the ducks. You feed the ducks, you're a criminal.

IRMA. (*flustered*) Oh! (*She thrusts the bag back into SAMUEL's hand and turns to stare straight ahead. After a moment she glances down to where Nellie is ob-*

viously clamoring for more. She reaches out her hand, and without looking at SAMUEL, demands:) Another piece of bread, please.

SAMUEL. It's all gone.

IRMA. (*imitating SAMUEL*) "It's all gone." (*to Nellie*) He says it's all gone. (*to SAMUEL*) You didn't bring enough. Look at them, they're still hungry. You want to feed them, feed them right.

SAMUEL. (*holding up the bag, he shakes out imaginary crumbs and begins to fold it carefully*) They're not hungry. They eat because they have nothing better to do. I feed them because I have nothing better to do. They're not hungry. (*He moves down center and squints out over the lake.*)

IRMA. I fed two children, I guess I know when someone's hungry.

SAMUEL. A duck's not a somebody. A duck is a duck.

IRMA. If they're God's creatures, they're somebody. Seven years?

SAMUEL. (*turning*) Eh?

IRMA. Seven years you've been feeding the ducks?

SAMUEL. Seven years. I began after my wife . . . The wife died, let me see, in 1975.

IRMA. That's six years.

SAMUEL. My wife died seven years ago.

IRMA. Six . . . (*counting on her fingers*) Nineteen seventy five to 1976, 1976 to 1977, 1977 to 1978, '79, '80, '81. Six years.

SAMUEL. Then my wife died in 1974.

IRMA. You don't remember when your wife died? Shame on you. (*to Nellie*) He doesn't remember when his wife died. (*smoothing her gloves*) My David died in 1970. Eleven years ago Oct. 27, may he rest in peace.

SAMUEL. (*walks over to the bench, seats himself on the*

far end from IRMA and looks out over the lake) You lost your husband?

IRMA. *(nods, also staring out at the lake)* God rest his soul. Forty years we were married. Forty years, two children and two grandchildren.

SAMUEL. *(sighs)* My wife died seven years ago. July, 1975.

IRMA. It was 1974.

SAMUEL. You knew my wife, Mrs. Know-It-All? You were there when she passed away? It was 1975!

IRMA. I know how to count.

SAMUEL. *(rising and crossing down left)* I come here to feed the ducks. I come here to close my eyes and sit in the sun. I come here every day for seven years, every day it doesn't rain, and today I meet Mrs. Know-It-All who tells me when my wife passed on! *(crosses stage right)* So I shouldn't be a criminal, I'm dropping the bag in the trash can. *(deposits the bag in the can)* So you shouldn't complain to the police.

IRMA. *(smooths her gloves, rises and crosses up center)* It's nothing to be ashamed of.

SAMUEL. I'm not ashamed of dropping a bag in a garbage can. Why should I be ashamed?

IRMA. *(turning)* You shouldn't be ashamed, your memory slips a little. People our age forget now and then. That's why I'm a little flustered myself. Maybe I should be going. *(starts to exit up left)*

SAMUEL. *(moving toward her)* You're a little flustered, you should sit down. At our age, you're a little flustered you better sit down and rest. *(He indicates the bench. IRMA hesitates, then returns and seats herself.)*

IRMA. Thank you.

SAMUEL. Rest awhile. *(He seats himself on the far end of the bench, and they both look out over the lake, their minds elsewhere. IRMA laughs softly. SAMUEL glances at her. A moment later IRMA laughs again.*) So I shouldn't feel so foolish, tell me what's funny.

IRMA. You have time?

SAMUEL. Time I have.

IRMA. (*opens her purse, takes out a pair of glasses and removes them from the case*) Sixty three dollars and fifty cents. (*passes them to SAMUEL*) Sixty three dollars and fifty cents for a pair of reading glasses.

(SAMUEL examines the glasses, nods sympathetically and returns them to her.)

For a pair of reading glasses . . . sixty three dollars and fifty cents. (*She puts the glasses back in the case and returns the case to her purse.*) A nice young man sold them to me in a store right down the street. A very nice young man . . . it wasn't his fault, the price. When he finished fitting me he had to fill out a form . . . my name, my address, the last time I was fitted for a pair of glasses, and my age. He asked me how old I was.

SAMUEL. You told him?

IRMA. It's a secret? Of course I told him. I'm 87, I said.

SAMUEL. (*turns and looks at her carefully*) My, my, my . . .

IRMA. His words exactly! "Eighty seven," he said, "my, my, my." And when he walked me up to the cashier he said, "This little lady is 87."

SAMUEL. Well, well, well . . .

IRMA. Her words exactly! She looked at me, and she shook her head and she said, "Well, well, well, that's hard to believe." I was half way down the street when it struck me.

SAMUEL. What?

IRMA. What I'd said! I marched back up that street and right back into that store and I said so everyone could hear, "I'm not 87," I said, "I'm 78!"

SAMUEL. (*gently*) So you forgot . . .

IRMA. Forgot how old I was!

SAMUEL. It happens.

IRMA. Oh yes, it happens. I know it happens. So you shouldn't feel so bad that you forgot when your wife died, may she rest in peace. (*sighs*) Seventy eight is old enough. Eighty seven, I don't need.

SAMUEL. I'm 79. Eighty, I don't need.

IRMA. Now eighty's not so bad. I have a friend who's eighty. She still lives in her own home, seven rooms, and she does very nicely.

SAMUEL. (*rises and crosses down right with a wave of his hand*) Eighty, I don't need!

IRMA. My friend could pass for 75.

SAMUEL. (*suddenly angry*) Another day I don't need.

IRMA. We all need another day. Tomorrow your son calls. Tomorrow your daughter asks you to dinner. Tomorrow you see the grandchildren. We all need another day.

SAMUEL. It was just my wife and me. The telephone doesn't ring.

IRMA. (*sympathetically*) Then tomorrow you make yourself a nice stewed chicken. A nice pot of chicken . . . a little onion, a little carrot and tomorrow's not so bad.

SAMUEL. (*picks up a crust and rolls it in his hand*) I eat in the diner down the street.

IRMA. You don't cook for yourself?

SAMUEL. No more.

IRMA. In a diner! Everything's fried in a diner!

SAMUEL. What's the difference, I don't taste it anymore?

IRMA. A nice stewed chicken you'd taste. Some dumplings, maybe, some fresh peas.

SAMUEL. (*crosses and sits down, his hands between his knees*) No, the diner's not so bad. They know me. The waitress knows my name. "Hey, Samuel," she says, "how are you?" It makes a difference, somebody knows your name.

IRMA. My husband had a cousin by the name of Samuel. He owned his own butcher shop. He knew a nice chicken.

SAMUEL. The waitress, she saves me the left-over bread. Saves me the bread for the ducks. Every morning she puts the left-over bread in a paper bag. "A little something for the ducks," she says. A very nice woman.

IRMA. This waitress, she's young?

(*SAMUEL shrugs.*)

Ah, she's not so young.

SAMUEL. (*irritated*) How should I know how old she is? (*He tosses the bread he's been holding to the ducks.*) Not eighty, that much I know. Eighty, I don't need. Tomorrow I don't need.

IRMA. (*gently*) Tomorrow will come whether you need it or not. You look to be a healthy man, a little thin, but healthy, so tommorow you'll be feeding the ducks, Mr. Criminal.

SAMUEL. I don't think so. (*rises, crosses down left and stares out at the water*) No, I don't think so. Not tomorrow. Not anymore. (*turning to her*) I've just been waiting for someone like you. A long time I've been waiting . . .

IRMA. (*offended, she rises*) I come here to catch my breath. I'm not looking for a gentleman friend, Mr. Fresh!

SAMUEL. And I wasn't waiting for a lady friend, Mrs. Know-It-All.

IRMA. So what were you waiting for?

SAMUEL. For someone with a way with ducks. Someone like yourself.

IRMA. Me? A way with ducks? What nonsense!

SAMUEL. Look at them. They like you.

IRMA. Nonsense.

SAMUEL. It's not nonsense. Other times I talk to people the ducks don't come near me. With you they're not afraid. Look at them. You have a way with ducks.

IRMA. I don't like ducks. I have no feel for ducks.

SAMUEL. Nevertheless, they like you.

IRMA. A duck in the pot I have a feel for. A duck in the park, I feel nothing.

SAMUEL. (*ignoring her comment*) That big one over there, that pig, her name is Nellie.

IRMA. Why tell me her name? I've forgotten her name already!

SAMUEL. Her name is Nellie.

IRMA. You want me to call a duck by name? Don't be so foolish.

SAMUEL. She likes the name.

IRMA. Fine. You call her Nellie. You be the old fool.

SAMUEL. I won't be around.

IRMA. Where are you going? You're so busy all of a sudden you can't feed the ducks? Six years you've been feeding them.

SAMUEL. Seven.

IRMA. Six years, every day it doesn't rain, you give them the bread. Am I right? So now you have some place to go, Mr. Busy-Man?

SAMUEL. I told you I won't be around anymore, not anymore.

IRMA. And I ask you, where are you going?

SAMUEL. (*tired of her probing*) I'm going, that's all, and you should feed the ducks.

IRMA. Why should I feed the ducks? He tells me he's going away. He won't tell me where, and I have to feed his ducks. Well, Mr. Traveling-Man, ducks I don't like.

SAMUEL. (*agitated, he crosses right*) It's not important that you like them. What's important is that they like you.

IRMA. Ducks I don't feed!

SAMUEL. Please . . . (*Scooping up her purse, IRMA begins to exit up left.*) No, don't go. I've been waiting for you . . . I've been waiting such a long time.

IRMA. Waiting for me, Irma Stein? Nonsense. See that sign? "Don't feed the Ducks." That means you – that means me.

SAMUEL. (*angry*) You would let them starve?

IRMA. I should go to jail so they don't go hungry? You feed them. You've been feeding them for six years.

SAMUEL. Seven! Seven years!

IRMA. (*her voice rising*) Six! Six years you've been feeding the ducks!

SAMUEL. Seven!

IRMA. Six!

SAMUEL. Please . . . Mrs . . .

IRMA. Six years you've been feeding them and no policeman! I feed the ducks I'll be arrested, wait and see. My little Daniel, you want he should have to tell his friends his grandmother is in jail?

SAMUEL. (*taking a different tact*) Look at her. (*He points to Nellie, then walks over to IRMA, takes her elbow and leads her down to the duck.*) Look at her, she likes you.

IRMA. Shoo!

SAMUEL. She doesn't scare easy.

IRMA. Shoo! Get away!

SAMUEL. I've never seen her take to anyone like this.

IRMA. So let her take to you. You like her, you feed her.

SAMUEL. (*crosses down left, agitated again*) I can't feed her anymore!

IRMA. Why?

SAMUEL. I just can't. It's your job now.

IRMA. My job? Tell me why it's my job.

SAMUEL. (*voice rising*) Because I'm tired. I'm tired, I tell you. I don't want it anymore.

IRMA. Nonsense. The way you talk anyone would think you're 97 instead of 79!

SAMUEL. I feel 97! One hundred, I feel!

IRMA. (*with anger equal to his*) The way you talk anyone would think you haven't a friend in the world.

SAMUEL. My friends are dead, ducks I have!

IRMA. Anyone would think you were good for nothing, a healthy man like you!

SAMUEL. What am I good for? I'm not even good for myself anymore!

IRMA. The way you talk, anyone would think you were better off dead!

(*There is sudden silence. The fight has gone out of
    SAMUEL. He turns slightly, refusing to look at
    IRMA. His shoulders sag.*)

Oh . . . (*IRMA is aghast. She moves to catch his eye,
but he turns away again.*) Ahhh . . . So . . . so . . . it's

Mr. . . . (*She can hardly say the word which she whispers.*) . . . Mr. Suicide, is it?

SAMUEL. (*staring stubbornly at the lake*) I have the right.

IRMA. What right? Shame!

SAMUEL. (*turning on her*) I have the right, Mrs. Know-It-All! I've lived a long time. At 79 the man has a right.

IRMA. Oh! (*to Nellie*) He says he has the right! (*to SAMUEL*) You have the right to eat in a diner and maybe ruin your digestion. You have the right to feed the ducks and maybe go to jail, but you don't have the right to take your own life. Only God has the right.

SAMUEL. No, I have the right! (*sits on the bench*) I'm tired. I've lived a long time and now I'm tired. I'm tired of walking up three flights of stairs to an empty apartment. I have the right. Me, Samuel, I have the right!

IRMA. You don't believe in God?

SAMUEL. I don't know. You walk up three flights of stairs and sit alone in the dark and after awhile you don't know.

IRMA. So turn on the lights.

SAMUEL. Why waste electricity? There's no one there to see.

IRMA. (*walking down right*) Shame on you. (*turning and pointing a finger at him*) And just how are you planning to do away with youself, Mr. Atheist? It's not as simple as you might think.

SAMUEL. Don't worry, I have it all worked out. I'll come here early in the morning, early, when there's no one around. (*rises and pantomimes the action*) I take off my jacket and I fold it and I put it on the bench. I take off my hat, I take off my tie, I take off my trousers and I put them on the bench. And I walk into the water.

IRMA. In your underwear?

SAMUEL. I should ruin a good jacket, a good pair of pants that someone else could wear?

IRMA. So that's your plan. I'm up here feeding the ducks, and you're out there floating in your underwear! (*waves an angry finger at him*) If I were going to do away with myself, God forbid, I wouldn't do it indecent. I'd lay down on my own bed and maybe take a pill.

SAMUEL. And die alone, three flights up in an empty apartment? No, I'll do away with myself here, with my friends, the only friends I have left.

IRMA. Self pity, it's very unbecoming a grown man. Make some more friends.

SAMUEL. I'm tired. More friends I don't need. I told you I'm tired.

IRMA. I'm tired, too, but I get up in the morning and I go out and I talk to people. I make a point of talking to people. Today I talked to the young man who sold me my glasses.

SAMUEL. And now he's a friend, I suppose?

IRMA. He's friendly, that's enough. And now look at me. I'm talking to a crazy old man who tells me he's going to do away with himself in his underwear. A skinny old man like you found floating in your underpants! At least you could wear a suit, God forgive you.

SAMUEL. It's a sin to ruin a suit someone else could wear.

IRMA. And doing away with yourself is not a sin?

SAMUEL. I'll have one sin on my conscience, I don't need two.

IRMA. And shaming your poor dead wife is not a sin? What would she think? Your picture in the paper, on the front page maybe, in your underwear?

SAMUEL. I'm not wearing my suit! This suit is real

wool. Fine wool. You think I would walk into the water in a fine wool suit? Wool shrinks. (*He holds out the edge of the jacket for her to feel, but she turns away. He follows her, holding out the material.*) Here, here, feel . . .

IRMA. (*She turns and reluctantly feels the material.*) Alright. Nice wool, I admit. (*walks to the bench and begins to pull on her gloves*) At least you could eat a good meal so you shouldn't look so skinny. For your wife, God rest her soul, you could eat a good meal.

SAMUEL. I'm not hungry anymore. Why should I waste good money when I don't taste the food.

IRMA. A nice stewed chicken you'd taste. You like chicken livers?

SAMUEL. What?

IRMA. Chicken liver. You like a little chicken liver?

SAMUEL. (*confused by the sudden turn in the conversation, he thinks a moment, then admits*) My wife made a very tasty dish with chicken livers.

IRMA. Your wife would ask for my recipe.

SAMUEL. My wife was famous for her chicken liver. All over the neighborhood she was famous.

IRMA. (*smugly*) Your wife, may she rest in peace, would ask for my recipe.

SAMUEL. (*turning away with a wave of his hand*) Ha!

IRMA. You don't believe me? I have a chicken in the refrigerator, a nice fat chicken, you come over tonight and you'll see.

SAMUEL. (*dismisses her again with a wave of his hand*) Ha!

IRMA. You've never tasted it like I make it. I promise it's a treat you won't forget. A real treat, believe me. And I have a special cracker . . . a little of my chicken liver on this cracker . . . (*She kisses the tips of her fingers to demonstrate the delicacy.*)

SAMUEL. Ahh . . . (*He senses her need to prove the point and slowly turns. He is ready to make a bargain.*)

IRMA. Then you'll come?

SAMUEL. Just a minute . . . you say that you want me to come over tonight?

IRMA. Yes, that's what I've been saying.

SAMUEL. You want me to taste your chicken liver?

IRMA. A real treat, you'll see.

SAMUEL. Alright. Alright, we'll make a bargain. I'll come over to your place and have a little chicken liver if you promise to feed the ducks.

IRMA. You mean I have to become a criminal before you'll taste my chicken liver?

SAMUEL. A bargain is a bargain.

IRMA. (*Irritated, she moves up center to consider, then turns.*) Alright, Mr. Stubborn Man, alright, I'll feed your ducks!

SAMUEL. You promise?

IRMA. I promise.

SAMUEL. Good. I'll tell them at the diner to save the bread. The waitress, she'll be sure to give it to you.

IRMA. I have my own bread. I can save my own crusts.

SAMUEL. A single woman like you, there wouldn't be enough.

IRMA. I won't go to any diner. Already I'm a criminal. Now you want me to be a beggar.

SAMUEL. I'll come over to your place tonight, I'll eat your chicken liver—but not unless you promise to go to the diner every morning, every morning it doesn't rain, and pick up the bread.

IRMA. Alright . . . alright . . . (*Now she has an idea of her own.*) But a promise for a promise.

SAMUEL. (*hesitant*) What?

IRMA. There's a nice couple down the hall. After dinner we'll play some pinochle.

SAMUEL. (*dubious*) I don't know . . .

IRMA. You want me to pick up the bread?

SAMUEL. Alright, a little pinochle.

IRMA. That's nice. That will be very nice. A nice dinner, a little pinochle. Eleven years I've been a widow and I still find I cook for two. I'm always giving food away. It'll be nice. I'll polish the silver.

SAMUEL. So alright, I'll bring a bottle of wine.

IRMA. That's nice.

SAMUEL. You like it dry, or you like it a little sweet?

IRMA. A little sweet.

SAMUEL. And now you should tell me where you live.

IRMA. I'll write it down so you shouldn't forget. (*Sitting on the bench she takes a paper and pen from her purse and writes.*) In the main building . . . I was one of the first tenants, my husband and myself . . . on the third floor, apartment five. I'll be expecting you a little before six.

SAMUEL. (*nodding*) A little before six.

IRMA. I have a deck off the living room. It's very pleasant. We'll sit awhile before dinner . . . a little wine, a little chicken liver. Then after dinner some pinochle. And tomorrow maybe you'll come over again. I have a fish . . .

SAMUEL. I'm not fond of fish.

IRMA. I make it very tasty. You'll like it, you'll see. You'll ask for my recipe.

SAMUEL. I don't know . . .

IRMA. If you don't come I'll have to give half of it away.

SAMUEL. In that case . . . (*He has a thought.*) Maybe a bigger bottle of wine . . . a little for the fish.

IRMA. A very fine idea. (*stepping back and looking at*

him) If you'd put on a little weight you'd be a very fine looking man.

SAMUEL. (*warmed by the compliment*) This suit is 100% wool. I'll brush it up a little. It will look like new.

IRMA. A very nice suit. I should know, my Daniel was a tailor.

(*SAMUEL extends the edge of the jacket again and she feels the cloth.*)

Very good quality.

SAMUEL. And I have a new tie. Well, not new, but I wore it very seldom. I'll put it on tonight so your friends shouldn't think I'm a pauper.

IRMA. My friends know quality. (*She pulls on her gloves and rises.*) So I'll expect you a little before six.

(*SAMUEL nods. IRMA begins to exit down left and SAMUEL begins to exit down right. He turns.*)

SAMUEL. A little lemon in the chicken liver. My wife always put a little lemon in her chicken liver. It made it very tasty.

IRMA. (*turns, offended*) I have my own recipe! I don't need anyone to tell me how to make a nice dish of chicken liver! (*Exasperated, she sets her hat more firmly on her head.*) A little before six. Try to be on time, Mr. Know-It-All!

SAMUEL. I should be late? I'm never late. I'm a very prompt person, Mrs. Criminall (*SAMUEL tips his hat in exagerated politeness. IRMA tosses her head and exits. When she is out of sight, SAMUEL reaches in a pocket and takes out a few bread crumbs he has secreted there and tosses them to Nellie. He seats himself on the bench and tosses her several more, then he stretches out his legs and, tipping his hat to the ducks in what is a wordless exclamation of joy, he rises and exits, whistling.)*

(The Lights Dim)

PROPERTY PLOT

(brought on stage by actors)

One paper bag . . . carried on stage by Samuel.
Black purse . . . carried by Irma.

COSTUME PLOT

IRMA wears a soft gray suit and black shoes. A soft yellow scarf is around her neck and a bright yellow hat perched on her head. She wears spotless white gloves and carries a black purse.

SAMUEL is dressed in a gray suit, black shoes and wears a yellow tie.

FLOOR PLAN OF SET

The stage is empty except for a bright yellow bench
left of center, facing the audience, a yellow trash can
down left and a yellow sign suspended from a wire
which hands up right. Black letters on the sign read:
DON'T FEED THE DUCKS.

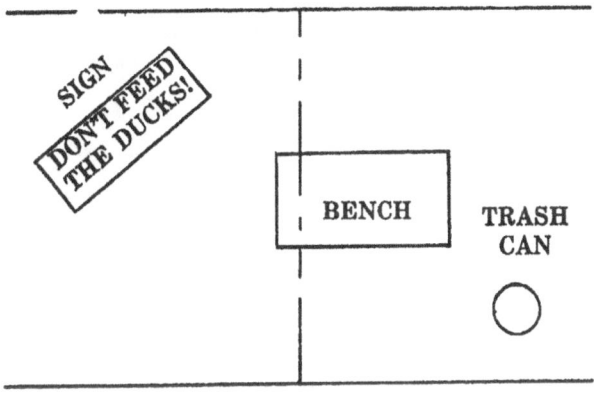

There are no other stage properties used in the play.

Scent of Honeysuckle

CAST

Jessie — *age 77*

Susan — *her mother (as remembered)*

Kate — *her daughter, age 45*

SCENT OF HONEYSUCKLE

SCENE: An old rocking chair sits in a pool of golden light. Up right of the chair and also in the lighted area is a table piled with an assortment of objects, including a tea canister and photograph album. A large cardboard box sits beside the table. Otherwise the stage is bare.

DIRECTIONS: As the play opens JESSIE is seated, rocking gently, eyes closed, a suitcase at her feet. She wears an old skirt of deep maroon, a spotless white blouse and a misshapen maroon sweater. She is a doughty old lady with a back as straight as a broom handle.

KATE. *(enters stage right)* Mama? *(She moves into the lighted area. A pleasant woman of 45, she wears maroon slacks and white blouse and carries a purse.)*
  JESSIE. In here.
  KATE. Ready? *(seeing the suitcase)* Good. *(picks it up)* It's a nice day for a drive. I'll carry your case.
  JESSIE. *(without opening her eyes)* Not going.
  KATE. Now, mama . . .
  JESSIE. Staying here.

KATE. Mama . . .

JESSIE. No.

KATE. Don't be foolish.

JESSIE. I'm not going.

KATE. Now mama . . . (*sets down the suitcase and places her purse on the table*) How about a cup of tea? A good hot cup of tea?

JESSIE. Had a cup of tea.

KATE. Well, I haven't and I'm going to put the kettle on. Where do you keep your tea bags?

JESSIE. Where I've always kept them.

KATE. (*picks up the tea canister*) In this old thing? (*opens it*) It's all rusted inside . . . (*carrying the canister, she moves out of the lighted area, stage right*) You're probably being poisoned with all this rust. It's a good thing you're getting rid of it.

(*During the following segment KATE is in what would be the kitchen. She mimes putting on the kettle and making a cup of tea.*)

JESSIE. I'm not getting rid of it, I'm not going.

KATE. How old is this thing, anyway?

JESSIE. How would I know how old it is? I can't remember how old I am.

KATE. Seventy-seven.

JESSIE. (*tartly*) Thank you.

KATE. Too old to be living alone.

JESSIE. Not alone, have my memories.

KATE. I'm not talking about memories, I'm talking about neighbors, people to pass the time of day.

JESSIE. When I need people I drive into town.

KATE. You can't drive, not anymore.

JESSIE. Why not?

KATE. They took your license.

JESSIE. Why would they take my license?

KATE. (*reentering lighted area*) See, you forgot already! (*mimes handing her mother a cup of tea*) They took your license after you knocked down Mr. Simpson's fence.

JESSIE. (*taking the cup*) Stuart Simpson is an ass. He's too old to be putting up a fence.

KATE. And you're too old to be knocking it down. Drink that tea.

JESSIE. (*taking a sip*) Too weak.

KATE. Drink it anyway, I want to get going.

JESSIE. Staying here.

KATE. Would you like to tell me how you'll manage? Half the time you forget to pay your bills.

JESSIE. Always pay my bills.

KATE. Sometimes you forget, then you forget you forgot.

JESSIE. (*rocks stubbornly, then stops; a pause; softly:*) I was born in this house.

KATE. (*gently*) I know, mama.

JESSIE. Lived here all my life.

KATE. (*patting her mother on the shoulder*) I know.

JESSIE. (*reaches up and takes KATE's hand*) You're a good girl, Katie.

KATE. I'm not a girl anymore, mama, I'm 45 years old. I have arthritis in my hands and I can't sleep on this shoulder at night because it hurts. I don't know why, but it hurts. I'm not a girl anymore and I can't drive 50 miles a day just to see you haven't taken another tumble.

JESSIE. No reason you should.

KATE. Every reason I should. I worry about you and I want you with us.

JESSIE. I'd be a bother.

KATE. I'm sure.

JESSIE. Two women in one house . . .

KATE. Is one too many.

JESSIE. I'm serious, Kathryn.

KATE. So am I. You're coming home with me. I'll toss these things in the box and we'll be on our way. (*picks up the photograph album*) How you loved to look through this . . .

JESSIE. Still do.

KATE. (*opening the album*) Musty . . .

JESSIE. So am I.

KATE. (*taking out a loose snapshot and looking at it*) Grandma? (*She shows it to JESSIE. JESSIE nods.*) She looks so young.

JESSIE. Came here as a bride. She was pretty but she was . . .

(*SUSAN enters stage left and moves to the edge of the lighted area.*)

SUSAN. Bowlegged.

KATE. What?

JESSIE. Said she was bowlegged.

(*SUSAN is the mother JESSIE remembers. KATE is unaware of her presence and does not hear her voice, which, of course, is in the mind and memory of JESSIE. When SUSAN speaks, KATE usually is turned from her, busy with the packing.*)

KATE. With the long skirt you'd never notice.

JESSIE. No sense packing. Not going.

KATE. (*ignoring her, picking up items and packing them*) It'll be nice . . . you'll like it . . . you'll have someone to talk to.

JESSIE. Talk to myself.

KATE. That's what worries me.

JESSIE. Just an old gray nuisance complicating your life.

SUSAN. (*shaking her head*) I can't get over that gray hair!

KATE. Why would you be a nuisance?

JESSIE. (*to SUSAN*) Well, after all, I'm 75 years old!

KATE. (*assuming the remark was directed at her*) You're 77, but what difference does that make?

SUSAN. Not a gray hair in my head.

JESSIE. You're 49!

KATE. (*straightening*) I'm 45, mama. I'm 45-years-old and running out of patience.

JESSIE. Not going.

KATE. Mama, the place is falling down around you! The window sill's rotting and look at the ceiling. Another year and it won't be fit to live in.

JESSIE. What's a little mess?

KATE. Oh, mama . . . (*turns back to packing*)

SUSAN. You were born messy, daughter. Used to sit in your high chair and smear everything in reach. Made your pa so cross. I finally set you in the sink and fed you there. Fed you right in the sink, and when you finished I held you under the faucet. (*She begins to laugh. JESSIE joins in, and SUSAN, who is dressed in a floor length maroon skirt and old-fashioned white blouse, moves to look over KATE's shoulder.*)

KATE. What's funny?

JESSIE. Something your grandma said.

KATE. You can't live with memories.

JESSIE. There's worse company.

KATE. And better.

SUSAN. I don't know about that.

KATE. Grandma's been dead 50 years. To hear you talk she's out there in the kitchen.

JESSIE. Sometimes seems she is. Out there in the kitchen, down by the creek, planting lemon verbena by the back step . . .

KATE. (*back to the packing*) And singing off-key.

SUSAN. What does she mean, "off-key?"

JESSIE. (*to SUSAN*) You never could carry a tune.

KATE. (*assuming JESSIE is speaking to her*) I take after grandma.

SUSAN. Not me. She's too bossy. She takes after your pa.

JESSIE. You're the boss in this family.

KATE. Me?

SUSAN. Fiddlesticks.

JESSIE. (*to SUSAN*) Yes, you.

KATE. (*rising*) Well, someone has to take charge.

JESSIE. Lead pa around by his nose.

SUSAN. Nonsense.

KATE. Who?

JESSIE. (*turning to KATE*) Your grandpa.

KATE. (*moving to her mother*) Mama, grandpa's dead.

JESSIE. Dead?

KATE. (*kneels in front of the rocker and takes her mother's hand*) Dead these 30 years.

JESSIE. (*She is silent a moment, trying to separate the present from the past for KATE's sake. [It makes no difference to her.] She pats her daughter's hand reassuringly.*) I know, I know, but sometimes it seems he's still here, swinging me so high, holding me so close seems I can smell the peppermint on his breath.

SUSAN. Your pa liked his peppermint tea.

KATE. You get confused, living out here by yourself. It's too lonely. (*rises to continue the packing*)

SUSAN. (*picking up the items to look at them as KATE places them in the box*) An old house is never lonely.

KATE. Forget to pay your bills . . .

SUSAN. A house has a spirit all its own.

KATE. Forget what day it is . . .

SUSAN. The spirit of the folks who lived in it.

KATE. Even forget your daddy died.

SUSAN. The women who washed and scrubbed and planted the garden.

KATE. (*turns to JESSIE, who is rocking gently, eyes closed*) And now it's time I took you home.

JESSIE. (*without opening her eyes*) I am home.

SUSAN. Every bit of life needs its own bit of earth.

JESSIE. (*repeating softly*) Every bit of life needs its own bit of earth.

SUSAN. Young folks don't understand, they transplant easy. Pull us up by the roots and we wither away.

KATE. The house is falling down around you!

JESSIE. (*stubbornly*) It's where I belong.

KATE. This empty old place?

JESSIE. Filled to overflowing.

KATE. With memories . . .

JESSIE. Real enough to me.

KATE. That's spooky!

JESSIE. Maybe. But when you're my age memories have texture and take up space. Close my eyes and I'm a girl again, down in the chicken coop tending my banties.

SUSAN. (*who has been wandering around examining the room, turns*) You don't want to spend your time down in the chicken coop, Jessie. (*She is talking to the lit-*

tle girl who once ran through these rooms.)

KATE. It's time I got you out of here.

SUSAN. You want to put on a pretty dress and go out dancing.

JESSIE. (*to her mother*) I'd rather stay home.

KATE. So you've said. (*Irritated, she turns and continues packing.*)

SUSAN. When I was your age I danced till midnight and rode home with the windows open and the scent of honeysuckle so strong it made me feel faint. (*begins to hum and do a little dance step*) To meet a man you have to get up and get out.

JESSIE. (*to SUSAN*) Well, I met a man.

KATE. Who?

JESSIE. (*to KATE*) Not talking to you.

SUSAN. Because you got yourself up.

JESSIE. (*to SUSAN*) Met James.

KATE. Daddy?

JESSIE. (*turning to KATE*) I said I met your pa.

SUSAN. Got yourself up and got yourself out.

KATE. (*Frightened by her mother seemingly talking to herself, she says soothingly:*) And papa would want you to come home with me.

JESSIE. Just like your grandmother, always pushing me out the door.

SUSAN. If it weren't for me you'd still be sitting here.

JESSIE. I'm still sitting here.

KATE. Because you're a stubborn old lady.

SUSAN. Stubborn!

JESSIE. (*to SUSAN*) Went, didn't I?

KATE. Went where?

JESSIE. (*to KATE*) Went to the dance.

KATE. What dance?

JESSIE. Went to the dance and met your father. Finally satisfied her.

KATE. Satisfied who?

SUSAN. Satisfied me.

JESSIE. Your grandma liked to see me stepping out . . . there was a dance at the grange of a Saturday. Pestered me so. I recall the night I met your pa. Your pa liked a good time, and I was a fair dancer. He asked to see me home, but the Ford was full so he stood on the running board and sang at the top of his lungs all the way.

KATE. Are you about ready to go, mama?

JESSIE. (*interrupting her*) Walked me to the door and said he was going to marry me.

KATE. We'll talk about it later . . .

JESSIE. "Certainly will not," I said. "I'm going to normal school and I'm going to be a teacher. "No you're not," he said, "you're going to marry me."

SUSAN. He was a good boy.

KATE. So I married him and we settled down here.

SUSAN. Had his faults but . . .

JESSIE. Don't say a word against him!

KATE. Why would I say anything against daddy?

SUSAN. See, you're upsetting the child.

JESSIE. *You're* upsetting *me!*

KATE. I'm sorry, I'm sorry, mama . . .

JESSIE. Not talking to you.

KATE. The doctor said to keep you quiet.

JESSIE. The old faker!

KATE. Remember your heart . . .

JESSIE. How could I forget, thumping away like it is?

KATE. See, you shouldn't get upset.

SUSAN. You're a stubborn old fool.

JESSIE. Says I'm a stubborn old fool.

KATE. He never said any such thing.

JESSIE. It's him who's the fool! Saying I have to leave my house!

KATE. He knows what's best.

JESSIE. Nincompoop!

KATE. You're the nincompoop!

SUSAN. Glad to see she has a temper.

JESSIE. (*to SUSAN*) Hush up.

KATE. I'll not hush up. Last time you had a spell you fell down the stairs.

JESSIE. Slipped on the bottom step.

SUSAN. Might have broke a hip.

JESSIE. Not talking to you.

KATE. Then for god's sake who are you talking to?

JESSIE. (*turning to KATE*) What?

KATE. Who are you talking to?

JESSIE. (*hesitates, shakes her head, then*) No one important.

KATE. Mama, there's no one here, important or not.

JESSIE. Don't be a know-it-all.

KATE. You said you feel faint.

JESSIE. No such thing.

KATE. Taking care of this place is too much for you.

JESSIE. It's all I know how to do.

KATE. It's time you did nothing.

JESSIE. When I have time to do nothing, I've had all the time I need.

SUSAN. Stubborn . . . from the day you were born you were stubborn.

KATE. The roof's leaking.

JESSIE. Is not.

KATE. When it rains it leaks.

JESSIE. Where?

KATE. *(pointing)* Up there.

JESSIE. Up where?

KATE. Right over your head, for heaven's sake.

JESSIE. *(looks up)* Well . . . *(settles back and crosses her hands)* When it rains I'll move my chair.

SUSAN. Stubborn . . . *(laughs)*

JESSIE. *(to SUSAN)* Not funny.

KATE. I know it's not funny. You don't hear me laughing. The paint's peeling off in the dining room.

JESSIE. I admit it's run down, but it's my home. Nourished me in the good times and nursed me in the bad.

KATE. Needs so much work . . .

JESSIE. I scrubbed the kitchen and tended the garden and made the best lemon meringue pie in the county cause your pa liked his lemon meringue.

KATE. Cost a fortune to fix up . . .

JESSIE. And in the afternoon, on toward dusk, I'd walk these fields till I knew every tree, every rock, every rise and dip of the land.

KATE. I'll be surprised if we find a buyer.

JESSIE. I had my dreams but they dropped away like my youth, so gentle I hardly noticed. I built my life around one man and lived my life in one house and I've no regrets. I never painted a picture and no one will remember my name, but I've been a happy woman.

SUSAN. I couldn't get you up and out, not really, but seems as if you're satisfied.

JESSIE. *(to SUSAN)* I'm satisfied, so why would I want to leave?

KATE. *(gently)* It's not a matter of wanting to leave,

you have to leave, mama.

JESSIE. Because I bumped my head?

KATE. Because you need someone to keep an eye on you.

JESSIE. Who told you that?

KATE. Dr. Reed.

JESSIE. Old coot should mind his own business.

KATE. Shame on you.

JESSIE. Set me in the sun and I won't ripen, I'll rot.

SUSAN. I just can't take it in, my little girl growing so old. And me without a gray hair in my head.

JESSIE. (to KATE) Your grandma passed on at 49 . . . not a gray hair in her head, if I'm to believe what she says.

KATE. If you hear grandma talking it's time we go.

JESSIE. Came home from the sanitarium feeling fine.

SUSAN. I wouldn't say I was feeling fine.

JESSIE. Dinner was over and she was shaking out the cloth. Passed away just like that. Had a hemorrhage, the doctor said.

SUSAN. I don't remember.

JESSIE. You don't remember? (She has spoken to SUSAN, but KATE answers.)

KATE. I wasn't there. ·

SUSAN. Doesn't seem important any more.

JESSIE. I only dreamed of mama once, dreamed I opened the dresser drawer and there she was, looking up at me and smiling. Isn't that peculiar?

(KATE shakes her head, kneels and begins to tape the box shut.)

SUSAN. Certainly is. If I was stuffed in the dresser drawer I wouldn't be smiling.

JESSIE. (*to KATE*) What do you suppose that dream meant?

SUSAN. Probably went to bed on a full stomach.

JESSIE. (*to SUSAN*) You're no comfort.

KATE. (*assuming this was meant for her*) I know, I'm a nag but it can't be helped. (*She continues taping the box. JESSIE sits forward, stops suddenly, holds herself rigid, then, after a moment, she leans back, takes a deep breath and closes her eyes. SUSAN watches her with gentle concern as she begins to hum softly and dance*)

SUSAN. The scent of honeysuckle so strong . . .

JESSIE. Open the window, Kathryn.

KATE. (*without looking up*) It's too cold.

JESSIE. I want to smell the honeysuckle.

KATE. In December?

(*JESSIE attempts to rise, stops again, holding herself rigid. Her face shows neither fear nor pain, it's as if she is listening to something within. SUSAN stops dancing and watches her a little sadly.*)

There now, packed and taped. (*She rises.*) I'll run down the road and fill the tank. Give you a few minutes to say your goodbyes. (*starts out, turns and comes back to rest her cheek on the old lady's head*) It's going to be alright . . . you know that, don't you?

(*JESSIE, eyes closed, reaches up and pats her daughter's hand. Reassured, KATE says with a smile:*)

You'll go quietly?

JESSIE. (*nods*) I'll go quietly.

KATE. Good. You see, everything's going to be alright.

JESSIE. I'm sure it is.

KATE. Now that I know you're going to be in safe hands, I can finally relax.

JESSIE. You can relax, daughter, I'll be in safe hands. (*She begins to relax, the slightest smile on her old face.*)

KATE. Good. (*She exits right. SUSAN, standing stage left on the edge of the pool of light, watches as the rocking chair slowly, slowly stops its gentle movement. The stage is perfectly still for a moment before she moves over to her daughter. JESSIE is motionless, the little smile still on her lips. It seems she is asleep.*)

SUSAN. Well now, that wasn't bad, was it?

(*There is no answer. SUSAN stretches out her hand. JESSIE remains motionless, but it is as if SUSAN is drawing her from the chair.*)

Time to get up, child, time to get up and get out. (*laughs lightly*) No, no, you look just fine . . . (*reaching out and smoothing back the hair on the unseen forehead*) But, oh, you were a messy child . . . (*straightens the unseen collar*) Made your pa so cross . . . (*arm outstretched, begins to draw the unseen form very slowly, very gently stage left*) Finally fed you in the sink, right there in the kitchen sink . . . (*Laughs, taking the unseen hand she has been holding and tucking it in the crook of her left arm, she moves out of the lighted area and off stage left, talking to that someone at her side.*) And when you were finished, just held you under the faucet . . .

(*The pool of light begins to dim until the motionless figure of the old woman in the rocking chair is in the dark.*)

PROPERTY PLOT

Properties on stage when play begins:

Items to be packed sit on the table, these include
... a tea canister and photograph album, also news-
      paper with which to wrap items for packing.
... a suitcase sits at Jessie's feet.

Properties brought on stage by a character:

... a cup of tea, brought on stage by Kate.

COSTUME PLOT

JESSIE wears an old skirt of deep maroon, a spotless white blouse and misshapen maroon sweater.

KATE wears maroon slacks and a white blouse and carries a purse.

SUSAN wears a floor length maroon skirt and an old fashioned white blouse.

Ground Plan of Set:

The stage is bare except for an old rocking chair sitting in a pool of light. Up right of the chair is a table piled with an assortment of objects, including a tea tin and photograph album. A large cardboard box sits beside the table.

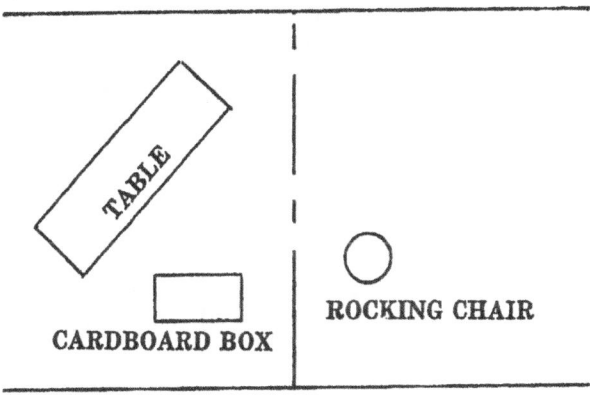

MUSIC USE NOTE

Licensees are solely responsible for obtaining formal written permission from copyright owners to use copyrighted music in the performance of this play and are strongly cautioned to do so. If no such permission is obtained by the licensee, then the licensee must use only original music that the licensee owns and controls. Licensees are solely responsible and liable for all music clearances and shall indemnify the copyright owners of the play(s) and their licensing agent, Samuel French, against any costs, expenses, losses and liabilities arising from the use of music by licensees. Please contact the appropriate music licensing authority in your territory for the rights to any incidental music.

IMPORTANT BILLING AND CREDIT REQUIREMENTS

If you have obtained performance rights to this title, please refer to your licensing agreement for important billing and credit requirements.